Hannah
the Happy Ever After Fairy

For Hannah Powell,
with lots of love and
happy ever afters.

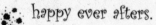

Special thanks to
Narinder Dhami

ORCHARD BOOKS
338 Euston Road, London NW1 3BH
Orchard Books Australia
Hachette Children's Books
Level 17/207 Kent Street, Sydney, NSW 2000
A Paperback Original

First published in Great Britain in 2006

A CIP catalogue record for this book is available
from the British Library.

ISBN 1 84616 252 1
1 3 5 7 9 10 8 6 4 2

The text paper within this book was donated by Abitibi
Consolidated Europe and Paper Management Services Ltd

Hannah
the Happy Ever After Fairy

by Daisy Meadows
illustrated by Georgie Ripper

This book has been specially written and published for
World Book Day 2006.
World Book Day is a worldwide celebration of books and reading,
and was marked in over 30 countries around the globe last year.
For further information please see www.worldbookday.com
World Book Day in the UK and Ireland is made possible by generous
sponsorship from National Book Tokens, participating publishers,
authors and booksellers. Booksellers who accept the £1 World Book
Day Token themselves fund the full cost of redeeming it.

ORCHARD BOOKS
www.rainbowmagic.co.uk

Welcome to Tippington Bookshop

Magic
Quill
Pen

Jack Frost's
Desk

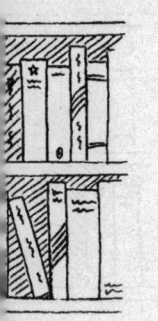

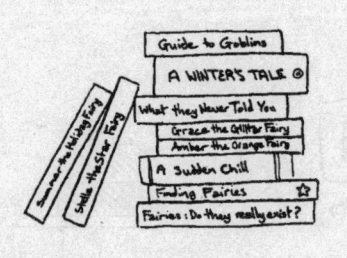

Guide to Goblins
A WINTER'S TALE
What they Never Told You
Grace the Glitter Fairy
Amber the Orange Fairy
A Sudden Chill
Finding Fairies
Fairies: Do they really exist?

Summer the Holiday Fairy
Stella the Star Fairy

Fairytale Shelf

Goldilocks
Hansel and Gretel
The Princess and the Pea
The Little Matchstick Girl
The Little Mermaid
Jack and the Beanstalk
SNOW WHITE
Lady & the Tramp
Sleeping Beauty
Rapunzel
The Three Little Pigs
Beauty and the Beast
Cinderella
Puff, The Magic Dragon
Ali Baba
Red Riding Hood
The Princess & the Frog

Children's Corner

Contents

Unhappy Endings

"Once upon a time," Kirsty Tate began, "there was a girl called Cinderella…"

Kirsty's best friend, Rachel Walker, smiled as she looked at the children in the audience. They were listening quietly to Kirsty, their eyes wide.

Rachel and Kirsty had offered to
read a story in the children's corner
at Tippington Bookshop, and now
they were sitting with the children
in the cosy reading area,
surrounded by shelves of books.

Kirsty went on with the story.
"'Oh!' Cinderella sighed. 'I'd love
to go to the ball!' But her stepsisters
glared at her and said…" Kirsty
glanced at Rachel who was doing
the voices of the nasty stepsisters.

"'You won't be going
to the ball!'" Rachel
said in a mean and
snooty voice,
making the
listening children
giggle. "'You're
just a kitchen maid
dressed in rags!'"

"Brilliant!" Kirsty whispered
to Rachel, turning the page.

11

"And Cinderella's evil stepsisters made sure Cinderella did not go to the ball," Kirsty read. "Instead, she stayed at home and cleaned the house, while her stepsisters had a wonderful time. They came home and told Cinderella all about the handsome prince…"

The children gasped in horror and Kirsty's voice tailed off as she realised what she was reading. Never before had she read a story of *Cinderella* where she didn't go to the ball! Flustered, she glanced at Rachel. Her friend was looking just as puzzled.

"Kirsty," a little girl called out,

anxiously, "how will Cinderella live happily ever after if she doesn't go to the ball?"

"Check the rest of the story, Kirsty," Rachel whispered.

Kirsty flipped ahead a few pages. Cinderella was still sweeping and dusting and her stepsisters were being mean to her. Even on the very last page, Cinderella was dressed in rags and her stepsisters were complaining that she hadn't washed their clothes properly!

"It's a different story," Kirsty
whispered to Rachel. "There's no
happy ending!"

Some of the children were
looking worried.

"Let's make it up," Rachel
suggested quietly to Kirsty. "After
all, we know what *should* happen!"

"Good idea," Kirsty agreed. She raised her voice. "So, on the night of the ball, Cinderella was sitting sadly by the fire. Suddenly, out of nowhere, there was a dazzling puff of glittering smoke!"

"It's Cinderella's Fairy Godmother!" the children shouted happily.

To Rachel and Kirsty's relief, the children didn't realise that the girls were making the story up as they went along.

"...and Cinderella and the prince lived happily ever after," Kirsty finished, and the children clapped.

"This book is really strange, Rachel," Kirsty said, as the children began leaving with their parents.

"I know," Rachel agreed, taking the book and flipping through the pages. "Do you think Charlie knows?" The girls glanced over at Charlie, the bookshop owner. He was busy at the computer near the till, but he looked up and waved at them.

"Well done, girls!" he called. "I'll be closing up soon, but you can wait here until Rachel's mum comes to collect you."

"Look, Rachel," Kirsty said, pointing at one of the bookshelves, "there are lots of fairytales here. Let's check the endings."

Rachel picked up a different copy of *Cinderella* and checked the last page. Again the story finished with Cinderella in rags.

Meanwhile, Kirsty opened *Rapunzel*. "Rachel!" she gasped. "Rapunzel's still stuck in the tower at the end of this story!"

Rachel was already looking at *Snow White*. She showed the last page to Kirsty. "…and Snow White was trapped in her glass case forever!" Rachel read aloud.

"All the stories have unhappy endings!" Kirsty exclaimed, flipping open *The Little Mermaid*. "Oh, no they haven't!" she corrected herself, handing the book to Rachel. "Look, the Little Mermaid does marry her prince!"

But as the girls stared at the book, the words seemed to blur and swim – the last sentence was changing before their very eyes! Now it said, "The Little Mermaid didn't marry the prince, and she didn't live happily ever after."

19

"This is very weird!" Kirsty gasped, reaching for a pop-up *Sleeping Beauty* book. "It seems like magic!"

"Yes, but it can't be fairy magic," Rachel added. "Not with sad endings!"

The girls knew all about fairy magic. They were friends with the fairies, and had helped them many times before when cold, icy Jack Frost and his goblin servants were causing trouble.

Kirsty opened *Sleeping Beauty* and a beautiful silver and blue cardboard castle popped up. The next moment, a glittering shower of silver fairy dust burst from the book and swirled around the girls. As the sparkles drifted down, Rachel and Kirsty saw a tiny fairy perched on the castle balcony!

"Hello, girls!" she called eagerly, waving at them.

A Sneaky Thief

The fairy flew up to join Rachel
and Kirsty, her blue dress floating
around her. She wore a daisy
chain necklace and belt, and
dainty blue ballet shoes.

"I'm Hannah the Happy
Ever After Fairy," she said, as
she perched on Rachel's shoulder.

"And I really need your help, girls!"

"No problem!" Kirsty said quickly. "What's happened?"

"Is it something to do with the unhappy endings?" Rachel asked.

Hannah nodded, her blonde ringlets bobbing. "I'm in charge of the magical Quill Pen in Fairyland," she explained.

"Yesterday Jack Frost sneaked into the palace and stole it!"

"What does the Quill Pen do?" Kirsty asked anxiously.

"It has the power to write fairytales for the human world," said Hannah. "But not only that — the magic pen can also change them!"

"Oh!" Rachel gasped. "So that's what Jack Frost's doing with the Quill Pen. He's rewriting all the endings of the fairytales to make them miserable!"

"Yes," Hannah replied. Her wings drooped and she looked very sad. "When Jack Frost writes an unhappy ending with the magic Quill Pen, every copy of that story in every bookshop, library, school or home around the world is changed! All he has to do is write the title of the story he wants to change at the top of the page."

The girls stared at each other in horror.

"That's terrible!" Kirsty cried.
"We have to stop him!"

"Yes, we must find Jack Frost
and get the magic Quill Pen back!"
Rachel agreed firmly.

Hannah smiled. "I knew
you'd want to help,
girls!" she said
gratefully. "But
it's going to be
very difficult.
We don't know
where Jack
Frost is, only
that he escaped
into the human
world with the Quill Pen!"

Just then the shop bell jingled as a customer came in.

"Charlie's just about to close, so that's probably my mum," Rachel said as Hannah hid behind her hair.

Hannah and the girls poked their heads round the bookshelves to see if Mrs Walker had arrived.

But, instead of Rachel's mum, standing just inside the door, and staring round the bookshop with an icy gaze, was Jack Frost himself!

A Cool Customer

Rachel and Kirsty could hardly
believe their eyes. Jack Frost had
used his magic to make himself
much taller, as tall as the highest
tower of the Fairyland Palace.
Icicles hung from his beard and he
looked more frightening than ever!
He carried a large bag, and there

were six ugly goblins with him.

Hannah put her wand to her lips.
"Don't make a sound, girls," she
whispered. "The Quill Pen must be
in that bag!"

Rachel and Kirsty watched as
Jack Frost stalked over to the till.

"I'm sorry, we're just about to close—" Charlie began, but then he glanced up and saw his new customer, and his mouth fell open in amazement.

Jack Frost raised his wand. "With this magic spell of mine, I freeze you here in space and time. When I leave you will be free, but you will not remember me!" he chanted.

Rachel and Kirsty watched in alarm as Charlie froze right where he stood, the look of amazement still on his face. Ice frosted over his hair and clothes, and long, glittering icicles hung from his nose.

"What's Jack Frost doing here?" whispered Kirsty. Hannah and Rachel shrugged, but just then Jack Frost turned to his goblins.

"I've changed all the fairytales I can think of," he told them. But there must be more."

He pointed at the bookshelves with his wand. "Find any which still have happy endings and bring them to me!"

Rachel and Kirsty looked at each other in panic. They were right in the middle of the fairytale section!

"This way, girls!" Hannah whispered, flying into the next aisle.

Rachel and Kirsty crept after her, away from the fairytales. Once out of sight, they peeped round the bookshelves to watch Jack Frost and his goblins.

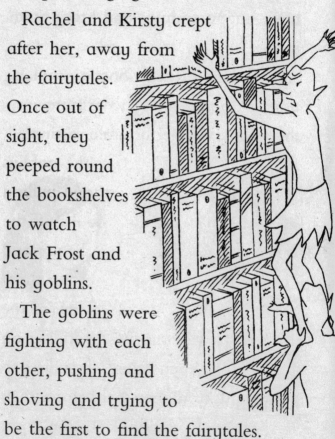

The goblins were fighting with each other, pushing and shoving and trying to be the first to find the fairytales.

"Get out of my way!" cried one. "No, I want to find a fairytale for Jack Frost!" yelled another. "They're making a terrible mess," Rachel whispered, as the goblins started pulling books off the shelves and tossing them aside. Some of the goblins were standing on each other's shoulders to reach the higher shelves and then throwing the books to the floor.

"Look at Jack Frost," said Hannah.

Jack Frost had made his way to the shop desk where he was now taking two piles of paper out of his bag. The girls could see that the pages in one pile had writing on them, but the pages in the other were blank.

Once the papers were arranged on the desk, Jack Frost opened his bag again and carefully drew out a long feather that glittered with all the colours of the rainbow.

"The magic Quill Pen!" Hannah breathed.

The Quill Pen shimmered in the shop lights as Jack Frost picked up a blank page.

"There won't be a single happy ever after left in any of the fairytales by the time I've finished!" he said, grinning nastily to himself as he began to write. Where the pen touched the paper, magical, multi-coloured sparkles shot in all directions.

"We have to get that pen back!" whispered Rachel.

"But how?" asked Kirsty with a frown.

Suddenly, a shout from one of the goblins startled the girls.

"This book's still got a happy ending!" the goblin cried, waving a copy of *Hansel and Gretel*. "I'll take it to Jack Frost!"

"No, I saw it first!" another goblin yelled, making a grab for the book. "Give it here!"

But the goblin holding the book dashed off towards Jack Frost.

The other goblin immediately gave chase, shrieking with rage. He threw himself at the first goblin and grabbed his legs, sending him

crashing into Jack Frost's
table. Both piles of
paper went flying.

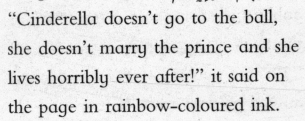

"You fools!"
roared Jack Frost.

One of the
pages landed
near Rachel, and
she picked it up.

"Cinderella doesn't go to the ball,
she doesn't marry the prince and she
lives horribly ever after!" it said on
the page in rainbow-coloured ink.

"These scattered pages must be
all the unhappy endings Jack Frost
has written with the Quill Pen,"
Hannah whispered.

"How can I get any work done with you idiots around?" Jack Frost yelled at the nervous goblins. He grabbed his wand, "So you cannot bother me at all, I hereby make you quiet and small!" he shouted.

A cloud of icy fairy dust streamed from Jack Frost's wand and filled the shop. It swirled around the goblins,

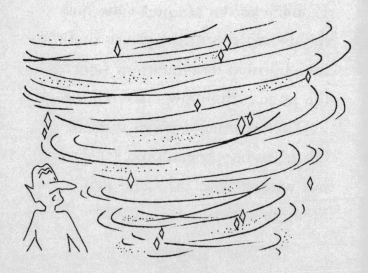

who immediately shrank to fairy size. Hannah quickly zoomed up to the ceiling away from the magic dust, but Rachel and Kirsty were caught in the spell.

"Kirsty!" Rachel gasped, as the magic dust cleared. "We've shrunk too!"

Kirsty looked at Rachel. "We're the same size as Hannah now, just like when the fairies make us small," she agreed, as Hannah flew back to join them. "But, look," she went on, pointing at her friend's shoulders. "This time we haven't got any wings!"

Girls Go Into Action

"What did you say?" Rachel asked with a frown. Kirsty's voice was so tiny and quiet, she could hardly hear her friend talking! It was only when she glanced over her own shoulder that she realised what Kirsty meant.

The girls stared at each other in

dismay. They had become fairy-sized many times before to help the fairies – but then they'd always had wings!

On the other side of the shelves, which now towered above the girls like skyscrapers, Jack Frost was picking up his papers and grumbling at the goblins.

"He's left the Quill Pen on the desk," Rachel pointed out. "Now's our chance!"

"Can you make us human-sized again?" Kirsty asked Hannah eagerly.

Hannah shook her head. "I can't undo Jack Frost's spell," she replied.

"That means that even if we get onto the desk, we can't pick up the Quill Pen," Kirsty said glumly. "It's too big."

"Well, I can't make you big, but I can make the Quill Pen small!" Hannah told her.

"Brilliant!" Kirsty sighed with relief. "But how do we get onto the

desktop? It's too high for us to reach!"

"Look," Rachel said, pointing to a stack of books on the floor. "Hannah, could you magic those books into a staircase?"

Hannah nodded and the girls watched as magic sparkles flew from her wand. The books immediately organised themselves into a staircase and Rachel and Kirsty ran over and began to climb.

"Nearly there, girls!" Hannah called encouragingly, as she fluttered above them. "Keep going!"

As she climbed higher, Rachel glanced over her shoulder. Her heart sank when she saw the goblins. They were jumping up and down and pointing – the girls had been spotted!

"Kirsty!" Rachel gasped. "The goblins have seen us, and they're trying to warn Jack Frost!"

Kirsty glanced at Jack Frost. "He hasn't noticed yet," she said. "He can't hear the goblins now they're so small and quiet, but we'd better hurry!"

Rachel and Kirsty stepped off the last book and onto the desk. They'd made it – and they could see the magical Quill Pen shimmering and sparkling not far away! But the goblins had given up trying to warn Jack Frost and were now climbing up the book staircase after the girls.

"They're coming!" Kirsty gasped. "Quick, Hannah, make the Quill Pen smaller!"

Hannah sent a swirl of fairy dust towards the pen, shrinking it to the size of a teaspoon.

"But the goblins are blocking your way down, girls!" she warned. "How are you going to get away?"

Rachel looked around desperately for an escape route as the goblins neared the desktop, but she couldn't see a way out. There was nothing on the desk except the Quill Pen and some blank pages, and the desk was far too high for them to jump off.

Suddenly, as she stared at the magic pen, Rachel had an idea. She knew the Quill Pen had the power to change stories, so what if she made everything happening right now into a story? A story called *Hannah the Happy Ever After*

Fairy. If she wrote the ending to the story now, surely the pen's magic would make it happen!

Quickly, Rachel grabbed the sparkling Quill Pen.

"What are you doing?" asked Kirsty, puzzled.

But Rachel didn't have time to reply. On top of one of the blank pages she wrote the title of her story:

Hannah the Happy Ever After Fairy.
But rainbow-coloured sparkles fizzed
from the magic pen as she wrote,
and the glitter of magic caught Jack
Frost's eye.

"Who's using my Quill Pen?" he
shouted from the back of the shop.

"Hurry, Rachel!" Kirsty gasped.
"The goblins have reached the top
of the staircase, and Jack Frost's seen
us and is raising his wand to cast
a spell!"

The Wind of Change

end, a fie
blew Jack Frost and
is far, far away!

"I've almost finished!" Rachel cried.

Kirsty peered over Rachel's
shoulder to see what she had written.
Under the title, it said, "In the end,
a fierce wind blew Jack Frost and all
his goblins far, far away!"

The moment Rachel finished
writing "away", Kirsty felt a strong

wind begin to pick up. Just as the
goblins stepped onto the desktop, the
wind whirled them off their feet and
swept them up into the air. The
goblins shouted in confusion.

Jack Frost rushed towards the desk,
pointing his wand at the girls. But in
a flash the wind scooped him up too.

"Put me down!" Jack Frost cried as

he was lifted off his feet and carried along helplessly on the strong breeze. "I'm the great Jack Frost! Put me down, I say!"

As Hannah and the girls watched, the shop door flew open and the wind blew Jack Frost and all his goblins outside into the street. Then it carried them off high up into the evening sky, still struggling and shouting.

"Well done, Rachel!" Hannah laughed, clapping her hands.

But Rachel was still writing. Curious, Kirsty and Hannah looked to see what else she had added.

"The fairytales got their happy endings back, and Charlie, Kirsty, Hannah and Rachel lived happily ever after!"

Immediately, Rachel
and Kirsty shot back
up to their normal
size and had to
scramble down
off the desk.
To their delight,
they saw that
Charlie wasn't
frozen any more
either. He was
typing away at the
computer, just as he
had been doing when Jack
Frost arrived. He gave the
girls a cheerful smile, as Hannah
ducked out of sight behind Kirsty.

"I expect your mum will be here soon, Rachel," he said, and disappeared into the stockroom. "What a relief!" Hannah smiled. "Jack Frost's spell means he doesn't remember anything. Now let's tidy up!"

She waved her wand. The girls watched as the books magically lifted themselves off the floor and jumped back onto the shelves in a swirl of glittering fairy magic.

"And if you ever need help with your own stories," Hannah went on

with a smile, "just come to
Fairyland and find me!"

"Thank you," laughed Rachel.

"Don't forget the Quill Pen,"
Kirsty said, picking up the tiny,
feathery pen and handing it
carefully to Hannah.

"Everyone in Fairyland will be
very grateful," said Hannah, her
eyes shining. "And so will everyone
who reads fairytales!
Goodbye, girls.
Thank you!"
And Hannah
and the Quill
Pen disappeared
in a cloud of
magical sparkles.

"What are you doing?" Rachel
asked, as Kirsty hurried over to the
children's corner.

"I just want to check," Kirsty
replied. She picked up the copy of
Cinderella they had been reading to

the children, and opened it at the last page.

Rachel and Kirsty beamed at each other, for the fairytale ended just as it should: "Cinderella married her prince and they lived happily ever after!"

Have you checked out the

website at:

www.rainbowmagic.co.uk

There are games, activities and
fun things to do, as well as news
and information about Rainbow
Magic and all of the fairies.

There are lots more Rainbow
Magic books, including:

The Rainbow Fairies
The Weather Fairies
The Party Fairies
The Jewel Fairies
The Pet Keeper Fairies

visit the website to find out more!